Waiting...
My
Valentine

RAJENDRA G

BlueRose
Publishers
NewDelhi • London

First Published in February 2022

ISBN: 978-93-5611-038-0

BLUEROSE PUBLISHERS

www.bluerosepublishers.com

info@bluerosepublishers.com

+91 8882 898 898

Cover Design:

Aveek

Typographic Design:

Rohit

Email Id:

rajendrag0019@gmail.com

Mobile No:

7385602336

Distributed by: BlueRose, Amazon, Flipkart

Dedicated To,

The CREATER of

The LOVE

Preface

This is my first story to be published as a writer. This story does not exalt or support any particular day. But the story has actually happened and the names and places in the story have been changed.

Reading the story will show that there was a special divine will or sign behind the story. The manifest discovery of the unmanifest God means love. It should not be bound by any place of caste and religion. God intends emotion and love is the cohesion of emotions. This story shows that if the feelings are pure, then God exists for sure.

If there is a will, there is a way and the fruit is obtained as per the wish, hence the direct message from this story is to avoid negative things and always pursue positive events, views. And I wanted to write this story consciously so that this message can be conveyed to all those who live by acknowledging the existence of God and experiencing God's grace like the hero.

Rajendra G

Acknowledgment

The ones who encouraged me to write this story were friends, Mr. Vinod Shinde, Milind Bansode, Pravin Bagul, Nandu Marke, Sagar Ghadge, Anushka Surve, Rajesh Kamble, Shalini Prasad More and Mr. Shrishail and always supporting the Big Boss Mr.Kashinath Sagumale are little to be thankful for.

Always encouraging me in my work my sister Mrs. Ranjana & Mr. Kalidas Gaonkar, Mr. Sanjay Ghadi, Mrs. Smita (Shobha) Santaji Pendhurkar, niece Shruti, Mrs. Shashi Deepak Chavan, and niece Tanvi.

Brother Mr. Padmakar Dabholkar provides information and guidance on computers, and the online system. Mr. Subhash Bala gave valuable guidance on story content and layout.

Mr. Ravindra (Babu) Gavkar, Mr. Dinesh Ghadi, Mr. Vijay Pendhurkar, Mr. Pramod Dabholkar always provide support in tough times.

A caring friend like Brother Mr. Dharmendra and Mrs. Falguni Joshi and a brother like friend Mr. Mahesh Mahadev Dabholkar and the one whose memories linger in my mind that kind brother, Late. Sharad. I will always be indebted to these all.

It is difficult to put into words the debt of my parents and wife Mrs. Vrushali.

Rajendra G

Friday: Today is a holiday for Raj, So Prince woke up late in the morning….. And took his toothbrush in hand, did some body stretching, and switched on the music system.

"On the Sky of heart, Shadow of sorrow is surrounded…

Missing you…. missing you…... missing you…."

As the music started, Raj's laziness ran away in a fraction of seconds. He freshened up while buzzing the song, his mother served him tea. He took the tea cup in his hand and got lost in song again…. After watching this, his mother got irritated and said,

"Today is a holiday, now for the whole day you'll annoy me by making me listen to these songs"

"Mother, I am not at home every day, to listen to the songs." Raj said in a upset tone.

"When did I say no to you Kido, you make me listen to these songs the whole day, that's just what I said…. Still better, your father has holiday on Sunday. Otherwise you know how he gets annoyed if you put on the music songs… " while saying this she went to the kitchen.

Then smiling himself, Raj went near the window…..at the same time the second song started….

"Not everyone here, doesn't get….

Love in life…."

And after hearing the words from the song, Suddenly Raj's mood changed, his face became serious….. Nervously he stared at the sky…… And he could see a figure clearly in front of eyes…. as bright and beautiful as a face of goddess in the temple. Raj felt the illusion that she is looking at him with her liner eyes…. And in that way he lost his mind, in her emotional stare….. Just like a movie of miraculous experiences….and memories started playing on the screen of his mind, which he had kept stored in the compartment of his heart for many years…

While taking a sip of tea, Raj's love story which is a long narrative story…… started taking shape in front of his eyes...

Raj, working as an engineer in a private company. His father is a government officer and mother is a housewife.

Everything is all right, but something was missing. Raj's mother wanted a daughter in law. So she was insisting Raj to get married, but Raj was not listening. Not even ready to see the girl, he was not ready for marriage. His parents, relatives, friends, everyone got tired of telling him. But he did not listen to any one. Whenever the topic of marriage comes, he gets lost in his thoughts…

Some years ago….. Friday was a holiday, and that was 31st Dec, the last day of year end.

Raj went to the corner shop nearby railway station, to buy items told by his mother. It was afternoon time…. He brought the items and came out of shop and he took mobile in his hand to call his friend to talk about the night's "New Year Party ". Meanwhile his attention went in front of him.....

One young lady with very beautiful and bright face was walking towards the station across the road..........Raj kept staring at her outstanding beauty and the brightness of her face........

She was wearing blue jeans and a white T-shirt, while walking slowly her silky hairs were free flowing in the air. Fair bright color, liner eyes, pink lips, energetic nose and smiling face like a goddess. And one more thing to remember is her "earrings" in ears which had gray-coloured beads alonwith silver chain... And it was moving rhythmically while walking along with her...

"Ear phone" to ears and mobile in hand.... Listening to songs while walking...... because her neck was also moving according to the music rhythm.... Seeing her charming and radiant appearance, similar to a deity in person... as you see in temples and you automatically gets diverted towards it, Raj unknowingly crossed the road behind her, walked towards her as if he was getting pulled... he was mesmerized by her glorious beauty.

At that time, he felt that she looked like modern goddess for today's era. And as any one like to taking the pictures of goddess in the temple Raj felt like taking her picture.....but with her permission... as it is wrong to take picture without asking her.

By thinking this with enthusiasm he went four steps ahead and suddenly stopped... He realized the reality when he saw people walking around him.

"What am I doing.... is it correct....?" 'If you like any one like this, it is correct to follow her....? And take her picture..... Even after asking her, but what if she misunderstood......and got annoyed and she creates a scene, then it will be embarrassment.... So doing this is foolishness.....' By thinking this way Raj stopped there.

Mumbling to himself.....' I liked her at first sight because her beauty is uncomparable, she is extremely beautiful...... every day so many girls can be seen while coming and going but like her, bright like a goddess, I saw today for the first time... and such beauty will empress on me, it is not true...... and overall attire and looks, definitely she must be a daughter of rich person.... But though I am not poor, and looking handsome still my living style is simple, so I can not afford the wealthy show like her, this is also very true...'

Raj smiled to himself, and mumble in his mind....."Let it go, I can not adjust with such a girl from a wealthy family..... Because of my simple lifestyle, and though she is looking like a Deity but how is her nature, what about her likings and choices? I don't know?"

What if we are a match with each other.... Then, but if.....if as per god wish, she is a part of my fortune.....if she has to come to my life, then she will be definitely can seen again.... And if that really happened, then I will talk to her for sure....

But for the first time, it is not by going behind her.... By saying this.... For a moment he looked at her, she was moving ahead.... Understood himself, He gave jerk to the body, turned to left... and went towards his house...

After coming home while sitting for a dinner, her thoughts kept coming in his mind...her bright looking face to her amazing beauty was seen before his eyes.... At that moment his friend called up to ask for a party at the night and his state of reverie got disturbed.

Raj's attention in the party was less. From time to time, her face was coming in front of his eyes, so he could not enjoy the party freely.

The next day Raj came to work. Her memories were fresh in his mind for first two days.... But slowly as the days went by, and at the end of the week, he almost forgot about her...

Today is a holiday, the second Friday has arised ... but so far she has been forgotten in Raj's mind, it has not been possible to remember her purposefully... Even then, while coming out, she suddenly peeked into his mind ... 'But now what does she look like again ... It's been eight days ... at the same time I should have spoken to her .... What's the use now, let's go ...' by mumbling this he went out.

Today, he wanted to buy clothes in market near to the railway station.

Late in the afternoon, after buying clothes from the market, he went to the station to go home.... He hurriedly reached the platform to catch the train, but the train was coming too late... so he had no choice but to wait for the train ....He took a mobile phone out of his pocket and at the same time, a young lady wearing a Punjabi dress with red and blue floral design ... earphones in her ears and mobile in her hand ... in such a state, the young lady came and stood near to the first class ladies compartment ... but Raj did not pay any special attention to her…

Looking at his mobile, as it was getting late to go home, he was waiting for the train to arrive ... At that moment, he noticed that young lady who was standing near to the 'First Class' was turning and looking at him...

Then he looked at her with easy curiosity... and while she seemed to look a little familiar, a thought came to his mind...

He saw a young lady last Friday…. Is she the same? ... But Raj got confused as the look of that young lady was very different in today's attire... On that day she was in a very modern look in jeans ... and today is in a Punjabi dress ... quite the opposite side. After looking at her only once, after eight days, her face was not well remembered by Raj ... so looking at her carefully, he started making sure that she was the same girl or someone else...

At that moment, his attention was drawn to her ear, and he was startled. In her ears same 'ear rings' with gray beads along with silver chain…. Which was in the ears of the young lady seen last Friday. Raj suddenly became happy by recognising her. Last time she had looked at Raj slightly, but today she was looking at him by herself. And, not only was she looking, but she also had a passionate feeling of love in her eyes... Raj was thrilled by the love in her sharp liner eyes.

He was so happy that, in the impulse of that joy ... he wanted to jump in the sky very high… he wanted to go very high and then hit the rising sea below, and reach the bottom of the sea directly ... filled with the divine pearls at the bottom. Leaping straight up in the sky again ... From the very height, looking down, at the head of the beauty goddess standing below, those divine pearls should be sprinkled... Such thrilling thoughts started stirring in his mind... he began to capture her supernatural beauty, radiant face in his eyes…

And her eyes ... the expression of love in her bright liner eyes, began to touch Raj's heart… he began to think that she would come forward and call him ... but she also must have felt the same way…. So, they just spent time by looking at each other like this...

Raj had a great aspiration in his heart... to go near and talk to her... to express his feelings but he had no courage... because Raj himself was handsome looking man, so many girls from school were always attracted to him... But since Raj's temperament was very shy since childhood, he never dared to talk to any girl, and if he ever dared to speak, he would get scared out of fear of anonymity... and he was not bold enough to talk, so he couldn't make any partners. And as Raj got old enough to get married, his parents started looking for a girl for him… According to Raj, getting married to an unknown girl directly was not appropriate… Because he think, the real happiness in the world was first acquaintance, friendship, then love and then understanding each other and finally getting married, only this ends up in real happiness for life...

But as per Raj's openion if this is true, due to shyness, he has never been able to make friends with anyone till the age of marriage today… and love was still far away…. In short, in terms of love, Raj was just as ignorant as Rajkapur in the movie 'Anaadi'.

At that moment, the train arrived and she entered the ladies first class and Raj in the back compartment…. While the train was starting, he decided in his mind... Let's get acquainted with her first after getting off at the station... if she speaks positively, then the next things can happen...

When the station came, the train stopped and then Raj started following her through the crowd of people.

When he got out of the station, let's go a little further and talk, while thinking this he was up the bridge.... In a short time he crossed the bridge and came out of station behind her.....

But he was left far behind by the crowd... he started running to reach her, and started walking very fast and reached near her.

When he was about to call her... Suddenly somebody patted his back from behind.... Now, who came in the middle...??? Raj turned back saying in his mind....

So 'Sandeep,' a friend from his neighborhood, came forward with smiling from... and when he saw him, Raj's heart felt consternation... but he recovered immediately, and smilingly said...

"Hi, Sandeep, you"

Hello, friend..... But today you came early from office ....?? Sandeep questioned.

"No, today is my holiday.... Went to market..." Raj said

"Yes, today is Friday, holiday for you... I forgot ... but it's nice to meet you, let's chit chat ... I'm bored to walk alone ..." Sandeep said...

"Oh yes ... let's go, let's talk ..." Raj started walking with him.

But from bottom of his heart, he was very annoyed. What are you going to do ... Let it be.... let's go, he said, and looked around while walking, to see her ... but he couldn't see her. She might have left.

After that, every coming Friday, she will appear like today and I will definitely talk to her today... by deciding this Raj would leave the house and... And surprise is that she would appear... but amusement is that it was just a co-incidence or miracle, this was not definitely understanding...... because her coming and going time was not decided and commutting way was also not fixed.

Sometimes in the morning, sometimes in the afternoon... sometimes near the station, sometimes far from the station... sometimes near another station, every time she would appear in a different place... but every Friday she would appear somewhere or other... so now seeing her every Friday without fail, Raj began to think that these were not just coincidences but divine miracles...

Because coincidences can happen twice, at most three or four times, but last five Fridays, it seems to be continuous... It is not possible in real life to have coincidences again and again without missing so many times. This happens only in movies, as written in the story... so she appears like this every Friday... when eyes meet she looks down and smiles as if she is familiar... And turning around and watching again and again with eyes filled with love... Raj was now convinced that her appearance and behavior was a divine miracle performed by God for Raj's marriage.

Sixth Friday.... Even though it was a holiday, Raj did not sleep as usual, Raj woke up early... He made a firm decision… some how I should talk to her today.... and without doing that he will not come home.

With great enthusiasm he went out of the house... but who knows what happened, Raj's determination was completely shattered ... she was not seen that day ... not at the station, not around the station... in the end after much frustration he even visited the crossroad where he has seen her the first time...

From that crossroad, and then, the Shiva temple that was seen while passing by ... he made a round at both the places.... but he could not see her. Then he came back and stopped near the station, but she did not appear....Today was a very bad day for Raj ... He came home with a sad face. The chain of divine coincidneces that has been going on for the last five weeks, finally broken today…

Raj came home dejected. So many thoughts were going on in his head… 'I had been seeing her for so many days, smiling ... looking at me ... but I kept silent ... never dared to speak to her. What will she do, and how will she take the initiative ... A man like me is afraid to take the initiative, though even she is a modern girl but she is from a good family... And if she had taken the initiative, I would have been suspicious of her character because of the male dominating cultural upbringing of mine... so it's not her fault, it's my mistake ... the truth is I didn't have the courage to talk to her. And what will God do… how many more opportunities will be given ... one after the other, continuous five Fridays... God has given me so many opportunities, by making so many coincidences continuously... but I didn't pay attention...

Continuously for five weeks, without deciding place or time, without missing, every Friday, automatically meeting somewhere or other ... what else to call this but divine miracle.... But miracles don't happen every day... Opportunity doesn't come again and again ... So now the coincidences are over ... Opportunity is gone ... There is no point in blaming fact...

Didn't even try... Forget it now..." Numerous thoughts made him upset. That night Raj was restless ... he couldn't sleep properly ... Early in the morning he slept a bit but the alarm started ringing...

He didn't want to go to office today ... but woke up because he couldn't get sound sleep. He did not have energy as usual so he reached office late. Somehow while working, the week ended in her thoughts, in her memories....

Today is the seventh Friday....Raj had to get up early as he wanted to go out of station for some work.

It was the usual time to leave the house, but since he had not seen her last Friday, he had a clear understanding in his mind that God had ended the series of coincidences. She will be not seen today or even in future as well.

Therefore, assuming that she would not appear again every Friday, the excitement with which he would leave the house was not at all seen on his face today... by looking at him, his mother was worried and said,

"Raj, don't you feel well? ... don't go then ... take rest today... instead of resting on holiday, you do some work every Friday ... you will fall sick because of negligence of health ..."

"No, mother, there is nothing like that, I am thinking, where to go first? ... Nothing else, let's go ..." Raj quickly turned his face and walked out ....After seeing that he had left, mother said ...,

"Go, but go slowly ... and come home early after finishing work ... do the rest of the other work later ..."

Saying "Yes ... I will come soon ..." by saying this he started walking down stairs....

After reaching the station, Raj bought a ticket and started walking towards the platform to catch the train. Last Friday she was not seen, and the chain of seeing her every Friday was broken, if she is seen today then I will definitely talk to her… but will she talk to me??....

And even if she talks what will she talk…. This pressure was not there now…. Because coincidence doesn't happen every day. And miracle etc... is not there….everything is a mind game…. he accepted this truth.

So he was walking freely towards his usual place to catch the train ... and at that moment, without any intention ... at the end of the platform, Raj saw a young lady walking in a black kurti and a dress with silver flower design. But he ignored….at the same time he felt that, after seeing Raj, she looked down and came forward… Along with that he stopped there for a moment.

And that was none other than his goddess of love. To make sure he turned his glance towards her direction…. and he was just puzzled…… he got a surprise. Was her… his love goddess…??

He had given up hope of seeing her again….. And when she was seen before him…… Raj's heart shook due to intense feelings of love. He thanked his fortune…. And one more coincidence or miracle..... But one more opportunity... As if God had given him one more chance.

She stood in front of the first class compartment and she also guessed where Raj is ... and as soon as she saw him, she started looking at him ... not once, again and again.... seeing that, Raj got encouraged with excitement.... Now this is the right time to talk and I should not waste the time....So he decided this and he stepped towards her direction...

Seeing him coming forward, a faint smile appeared on her face.... On seeing this Raj became happy....

But as he got closer, she looked down and bowed her neck ... so Raj couldn't look into her eyes and communicate with her...

As he looked at her bowed face, he walked in front of her and stopped in front of next compartment... She turned her head and looked at Raj ... Raj was looking at her ... And then she glanced at Raj again.

But when it was time for the train to arrive, the crowd of people increased, so how can he speak in front of so many people ... People will look at us with suspicious thoughts ... this thought made Raj awkward and lost in his thought....but she was looking at him by turning her neck with her sharp liner eyes... But due to the crowd of people, Raj did not dare to go forward....

Raj went halfway and in a few steps, he was about to reach her, a train arrived on platform ... to catch the train, people started running from here and there towards the coaches .... Raj could not go further any more.

She saw that Raj stopped again, she turned around and saw towards the train, her compartment came near her ... She looked back again at Raj but as the trained stopped, people rushed to enter the train, so she could not see Raj nor Raj could see her as well.

Finally, realizing that she must have caught the train, Raj promptly got into the front compartment, but he tried to look back while entering into the compartment to see if she is waiting on the platform or she too had caught the train. But due to the crowd he could not see well, and the train picked up speed…

Later, as soon as the next station came, Raj stood near the door to see whether she was getting off or not, he started looking for her in the crowd of women returning back from train...

But even after crossing through three or four stations, Raj could not see her again... And then due to the large crowd, Raj had to enter into the train... Finaly Raj had lost the opportunity given to him by God once again... and from the agony of his mind came out a song on his lips...

"in the journey of life, who goes away, achievements…..

Those, doesn't come again….. Those, doesn't come again…"

Song was coming from bottom of the heart, so he was not bothered about the environment around, and started singing loudly… and neighbours started looking at him a bit strangely. As soon as he realized that, Raj stopped singing. He closed his eyes to hide the pain on his face and started thinking…

With this situation, He stood in the crowd for a long time… All the events from the first Friday to the seventh Friday till today were playing in his mind like a movie ... and he was blaming himself again and again…

The desired station came.... Raj got out of the train, and looked at the womens coming out from previous compartment with hope.... to see her, but she was not seen.... Then he stopped till the time the train started and thought after the train starts, "I will check in compartment if she is there".... but, invain, he didn't see her... at last he was embarrassed and went further...

Raj returned home after finishing his work, but there was no enthusiasm, his mood was very upset…. He was imagining the morning scene in front of his eyes...

"Just before the train arrived, what would have happened if I had gone to her and talked to her…?? What is the point in talking now? Time has gone… I don't know if I will ever see her back. Don't know …" With this thought he reached home from station.

When he reached home, his mother would look at his sad face and ask questions… so as soon as she opened the door, hiding his face he ran to the washroom. After having dinner he went to sleep but for long time he was restless…..

On the second day Raj went to the office somehow… While entering into the office his colleague 'Akash' asked him after seeing his contemplative face,

"Raj sir, is there any problem ... you look very upset ..."

"No, there's nothing like that." Raj said with changing the expression of his face.

"What nothing?" The face is saying something is wrong…??
"

Akash winked mischievously.

“Nothing, nothing is wrong…… We will talk in evening…” Raj said this while going to the boss’s cabin.

After the staff left from thc office in the evening, Raj told everything to Akash about whatever had happen in the last few days. Now because his mind was suffocated. So, it was important.

Akash was younger than Raj but he was successful in terms of love. When he heard Raj's series of so many coincidences, he said with a smile ....,

"Sir, what kind of coincidences .... If I would have been in your place, then I would have spoken to her at the second or at least at the third chance, I would have opened up my mind and spoken to her freely ... and you have remained silent for so many days ... you have not said anything....?? ”

"It's not like that, at first time I didn't feel right to talk ... and then whenever I went to talk, there were hurdles ..." After saying this, Raj explained in detail how he had encountered difficulties while talking to her till now. After listening to his story, Aakash said while thinking in mind...

“Sir, I have an Idea, If you agree it...

“Then tell me fast, what I do…. so she can understand my love…” Raj said while getting excited…

"Sir, you do one thing, next Friday I will come with you ... and if we see her again then I will talk to her and will set the meeting for both of you ..." Akash told his idea....

“Ok, will do that… if you say so….” Raj said with consent.

Though Raj showed his consent, still he was reluntant internally.... Because due to Akash mediation, his work may happen..... But one will make love and other person will help to be achieved it, this thing was not convinced to Raj. By this thought he became serious again, he was not able to think anything. He closed his eyes and started thinking in his mind.... And suddenly, he remembered.... He found the way.... to express his love... A new opportunity had arisen.... so Raj, who does not remain silent by acepting defeat, was once again excited with new hope...

That opportunity was... Coming Monday, three more days later... the day which brings the world lovers together... the 'Valentine's Day'..... It was a big opportunity for Raj...and he decided not to waste that opportunity...

After finishing his dinner fast ... Raj wrote a letter to her at night... All the incidenets from the first Friday when she appeared before him, till the seventh Friday ... And so, how madly he is now in love with her... One page for each Friday ... seven pages on the whole he wrote ... and at the end, he wrote his name and mobile number..... While coming home Raj brought a CD of new love songs that she would like it. Keeping in mind that she always listens to songs with earphones in her ears.

The name of the album of those songs was also very suggestive, 'Don't feel anywhere, without You...' Inside the CD cover, Raj kept his love letter neatly and made an attractive gift pack.... while thinking how to gift this the coming Valentines Day, he instantly remembered...

She had caught the same time train twice on the last Friday and earlier once before that... Considering that she was always going to college at the same time, and assuming that she would go to college at the same time on Valentine's Day… Having decided to meet her at that time, Raj slept peacefully in joy…

Monday, today is 'Valentine's Day'... a day to express the love that lovers all over the world are eagerly waiting for… like them, today Raj too was eager to celebrate his 'Valentines, Day'....

So he got up very early in the morning ... and listened to his favorite songs ... 'Today she will meet me definitely and I will celebrate my Valentine's Day after so many years….' By this thought he was delighted…. and seeing his enthusiasm, mother asked....,

"Raj looks very happy... what is the amusement son, what is the plan which you are not telling your mother...?"

"Mom, not now .... I'll tell you when it's done... surprise..." Raj said excitedly....

"Very nice…. Things will happen as per your wish…. I am waiting for your surprise…" Mother said happily….

As he was getting ready, Raj called his office and informed that he was taking halfday leave from office... and after saying goodbye to his mother, he came out smiling with a happy face....

According to Raj, if she goes by train before her usual train, the day will be missed ... So Raj reached the station an hour earlier and started waiting for her near her usual first class coach ... How to give her the Valentines gift…he thought while waiting... he started thinking about what to say to her....

An hour has passed ... many trains passed ... she did not arrive.... finally, it was time for her usual train to arrive.... Raj’s longing increased as time came… his eagerness increased to meet her…..He started looking at the indicator and the direction of her arrival ... but she was not coming....

Even though it was announced that the train was coming, but she had not arrived, Raj's was no more curious... now there was a look of concern on his face.... he became serious, then the usual train arrived ... people started running to catch the train... So, Raj started looking at the people running with wide eyes…

Because maybe even when the train was starting, she would come and catch the train and leave ... but no ... the usual train also came.... but she didn't come ... then Raj got nervous.... but may be she would go by other train later…. With that hope he started waiting for her...

Many trains have passed.... an hour has passed while waiting ... trains had come and gone... but she had not come, she had not…..

"Now it is afternoon, how much long I should wait ... I informed in the office that I will take a half-day, now if I don’t reach office on time, boss will scold me ... Come on, she is not coming now ..." And he caught the train with heavy steps ...

While travelling in the train, he was thinking about why she did not come today, and he suddenly noticed one thing.... which made him very happy ... he realized that some of the beautiful girls going to college must have a boyfriend ...And he is probably from the college… and if she had a boyfriend, she would have gone to college today to celebrate Valentine's

Day... but she didn't go to college today, that means she is still single…

And one more thing, he was convinced that she is single... that is, every Friday for the last two months, whenever she appeared, she was alone or with a couple of girl friends ....But in all those days, when she was alone or with her girl friends, he never saw any boy with her ... and both of these things came to his mind, even though she didn't come today.

He hadn't celebrated Valentine's Day, so he was sad for a while ... but she is still single and that's why I like her, these thoughts made him happy though he was sad.

"Sir, I think you have celebrated your 'Valentine's Day'????..." Receptionist Sunita Madam asked him while entering into the office

"What 'Valentines' ... the company and the boss ... and who is ours ..." Raj said smiling.

But even if he was smiling outside, internally he was in pain which only he knew…. So instead of giving wrong answers to others and increasing the tension… he took the file and went to the boss's cabin…. He was not able to pay any attention at work, and some how the day was over….

Raj was still awake at the night.... but there was no restlessness as before, When he was on the bed... he took the CD gift of 'Don't feel anwhere, without You…' album that was for her, took it out of his pocket and listened to all the songs on headphones again and again, waking up in the night in her memory ....

He was sad by one thought that he had not met her today, but by another thought he was happy to know that she was still single and that why she likes me ... this feeling made him happy… at the end he could sleep only early in the morning…. Due to this he could'nt attend office that day.

He woke late afternoon, after lunch he listened that songs CD once again till the time his spirit was full of happiness, and later he copied all the songs from the CD…. and kept that CD along with the love letter in the internal pocket of his office bag.

After that every on Fridays, Raj went out for some work without fail before coming home… the shop where she was seen on the first Friday, and then the next Friday, on the road near the Shiva temple, he made a trip round. With the hope that she would be seen somewhere ... but if she is not seen, then he will explain to his mind ... at least he would go to Shiva temple and pray for his parents and for her and then only he would go back home ....

Years went by... but Raj's never missed his Friday rounds... and he never saw her again… yet Raj had full faith in his love. He was sure that she would be seen again one day, today, tomorrow, the day after tomorrow, one day or another... but she should not be forgotten during this time...

He made it a point so that her face would not be forgotten as he had not seen her for many days... so that she would be remembered every day and his love for her would remain in his heart.

'If there is will there is a way' and you will get the fruits as per your wish by the laws of nature and some of his own experience in this regard, with the passionate love for her and the intense desire to visit her, he will definitely meet her... He kept the password of his Facebook account: 'Friday Valentine'.

And then every evening after office duty, he would open his Facebook account with that password and start searching for her.... but she was not found on facebook either ... And her memories were getting darker in Raj's mind ....

After finishing one year, another started... and in the second year... the events that happened before that can be called a coincidence without being called a miracle… but it has to be said that the events from this time were a miracle...

On that Friday evening, Raj had finished his day's work and gone to the Shiva temple, as usual, walking on both the paths for his love deity.... He prayed for his parents and her, and started walking towards the station to go home ... he must have taken a few steps…..

Suddenly, on the other side of the road, there was a young lady who looked like her, or the same.... Raj saw walking back towards the Shiva temple ... he saw her or it was just his illusion ...who knows?.....he stopped immediately and turned back and tried to see clearly... but because of the crowd on the road, he couldn't see her...

He felt like he had made a mistake. Whether it was her or someone else…… or else I just had an illusion. With this thought Raj returned home… but he decided in his mind…

The next Friday at the same time he would go to the Shiva temple, pray to Lord Shiva for her visit and wait near the temple until she meets him... If my love for her is real, then surely God will make her meet me.

Today, two years later, he woke up on Friday, and from the time he woke up in the morning, his eyes were waiting for the evening time… and as soon as the evening time started, Raj reached Shiva temple with his love story ...and he prayed to the Shiva statue in true mind….,

O God, My goddess of love, whom I am searching from last two years, To meet her I am desperate….. Last two years ago I couldn't see my goddess of love, Almighty with your grace, I should be able to see her today without fail…. And as usual instead of only seeing her, I should be able to speak to her directly…. God please accept my prayer of pure love. Help me God… Let me be enlightened by your grace.... let my love goddess appear infront of me today, let me speak to her..."

After heartfelt a prayer Raj stood out of the temple…..to wait for her…. Because today he had a feeling in his mind that she will appear… So he became impatient and eagerly waited for her to appear.... Half an hour passed.... An hour passed.... but she did not appear.... But Raj had decided today ... that without seeing her, without talking to her he will not go home.....

After one and half hour, he did not see any sign of her appearance..... He was still standing firmly.... Just then he received a call from his father, "Did you show your mother's medical report to the doctor?" ... And Raj hit his hand on his head…

When Raj came from home, he had forgotten that his mother had given her medical reports to be shown to the doctor… if I don't go to the doctor, hospital will be closed and father will get angry.... after this thought came to mind, he just glanced at the road, in the direction which she was expected to come from…. But she was not seen. So, first let's go to the doctor and come back…. with this thought he turned his look towards temple direction and said,

"Lord, when will your grace come ... I have waited for a long time..... But how can I meet her today ..." he said and went to the doctor.

After showing the mother's report to the doctor and taking the medicine prescribed by the doctor, Raj went back to the temple ... An hour had passed by then and now it was time for dinner.... So, if I get late in returning home, father will get annoyed, so lets not wait for more time, last try, let's see if I can see her while going….

If there is grace of God, she will be seen ... and if not seen, then this subject is closed forever ... I don't want to think about it again. Just a trouble to mind ... Saying this, Raj reached near the Shiva temple ... and looking at the Shiva statue inside the temple from outside, he said,

"Almighty god you don't have a wish to show me my love Goddess. She should speak to me…..you know all my pain… and still you are not showing your grace to me…. I am angry at you ... If you think that my love is pure and holy, then make me meet her ... What more can I say to you ... I will come back ... "Saying this, he looked at the Shiva statue for a moment and moved on to go home...

After walking a little further, the road in front appeared to be dug horizontally ... but in the evening when he came to the temple, the road was in a good condition... now suddenly someone had dug at night, thinking that…

He saw further, the dug pit was big ... so it was difficult to cross the pit, so he turned right and came to the road on the other side and went four steps ahead, he noticed the front and… he missed his heartbeat...

In reality, Raj's love goddess, who appeared every Friday had now appeared before Raj ... She looked like a goddess due to her radiant supernatural beauty.... As usual, tunned to hear the songs on the 'earphones', was coming forward with slow steps.... and while walking, her identity mark. ... The gray beads along with the silver chain of the 'earring' in her ear, was moving back and forth along with her moves....

Seeing her in front of him all of a sudden, Raj couldn't believe his eyes at first.... so, he really pinched his hand to make sure... that this is not a dream.... but it was the truth... the truth was created by Shiva, it was a miracle...

On the one hand, he was very happy, on the other hand, he was staring at her with his full open eyes and due to the enormous pressure his heart beat became fast. But Raj was so overwhelmed by the experience of that miracle that she even came in front of him and went ahead...

She was busy in hearing songs on 'ear phone', her attention was not there around. When she went back then Raj's mind became alert… The Lord had really heard his prayer... His grace had been shown...

Raj was anxious to see her from last two years, but today, by the grace of God, she appeared in front of him in just two hours…. Overwhelmed by this feeling, he mentally remembered Shiva... bowed from the heart...

And after recovering... he went forward in excitement to talk to her ... walking, fastly, he reached close to her… gathered all his courage and said...,

"Just a minute…."

She must have not heard Raj's words because of the 'earphones' in her ears ... so she started moving forward ...

seeing that, he immediately walked ahead and looked at her and Raj again said,

"Just a minute ..."

When she noticed that the person walking beside her was asking her something ... she stopped ...and after stopping she removed 'ear phones', and said in her sweet voice

"What is it…?"

Today was the first time Raj had heard her voice since she started appearing two years ago…. He was overwhelmed by that voice ... Her soft and sweet voice was very similar to her supernatural radiant beauty ... While trying to retain that sweet voice in his ears, he came to his senses...still does she know me or that she has forgotten me in two years. Raj questioned to check that..."

"Do you recognized me…?"

"No…" she said with the same tenderness…..

As soon as he heard that, Raj felt ashamed. The thought that she did not recognize him suddenly choked his throat.... Words wouldn't come to his lips ... Thinking about what to say, he quickly told the previous incidents to help her memory…

"Every Friday… two years ago, that's how we meet ..."

But as soon as she heard that, she said, "Sorry… " and started walking...

However, after hearing the word 'sorry'.... Raj became weak ... instead of stopping her, he just kept looking at her while she was leaving ... Thoughts flooded his mind...'She'… is saying Sorry and walking without stopping..... It means she doesn't recongnise me anymore ... or even knowing me, that I didn't take the initiative at that time, so now she is angry and leaving me.....

That someone else has come into her life because we haven't met in the last two years… so she said 'sorry'..... what it means, what is the meaing of that 'sorry...' what to do now ... Should I ask her to stop and request her to listen to me, but ... will she stop now .. ?? And if she stops, will she listen ... if she doesn't listen ... and if she says she doesn't know me, then maybe if she misunderstands and shouts....??'

Raj was not getting any idea.... She was moving forward and he was standing there stunned ... The distance between her and Raj was slowly increasing.... In the same regretting state, he looked at her fading figure...

Before Raj's eyes, the last incident of Kamal Hassan's 'Sadma' movie played.... The heroine who behaves like a child despite coming of age due to amnesia, heroine completely forgetting her past…. Despite being in the company of the hero for a year, as soon as she rccovers, she catches the train along with her mother and father to go home, when hero comes running to meet her at the station… But the honest hero who took care of her all year round and loved her dearly while caring for her, at that time she did not know him at all... she doesn't remember the service he rendered to her during her illness….

So the hero, in order to awaken her memories... to keep her happy in her sickness... plays the usual crazy ... childish games and imitations with her ... but she doesn't remember anything... and he becames a stranger to her now….This man is doing something crazy, which means he must be a crazy beggar and he is hungry but can't speak… thinking that ... she throws some food at him from the window of the train… and train starts…..

At that moment, the hero is crying ... he is really in a state of madness …hero who understood that her lost memory was back again, of which he was not part of it. … So not even if he tries hard to hit the head, still she wont be able to recognize him… and then…..with this feeling… The hero, distressed by this realization, turns back in despair.

Journey of the heroine beginst where memory about hero is not recollected.... Never to meet the hero again.... even after understanding the reality, she might have turned back to see him… with this false hope hero turns back towards train,

But his eyes fill with tears, so he could not see the train cleary… and suddenly recovering from that big shock ... wiping his eyes, the hero slowly walks back.

'Sadma' means a big shock to the mind... which makes it very difficult to recover... this is the unfortunate end of the movie, which Raj did see many times by replaying it on the video player, over and over again during his college days.... he had seen so many times….

And at that time, it was as if he was in harmony with the sad feelings of the hero of the movie.... Therefore, today, maybe, as he had wished, it bore fruit according to this law of nature.... Raj laughed for a moment at this strange game of destiny..... And next movement like the hero of Sadma, his eyes filled with tears….

Now she had gone far beyond stopping... and now ... like the heroine in 'Sadma'.... Maybe she too will never be seen again, accepting this fact ... to see her once last time, Raj rolled his eyes. Turned to look at her direction...

And going further his goddess of love, He looked for a moment at the figure behind, which looked unclear due to tears....

As she disappeared, tears from his eyes.... Cleaned with the click of a fingure... Raj smiled mischievously to shake off the sadness in his heart, Raj turned back ... and while walking, the sad song from the movie 'Sadma' started playing in his mind...

"hey life, meet me..... even I have accepted you... every part of sad life...

Accepted it.... Yes, hey life meet me..."

As the words of the song were intertwined with the emotions of the mind, Raj became one with the hero of the movie and started singing loudly ... and while singing the song went straight into the heart of this hero ... as if he was no longer in the real world, but in the movie story on the screen .... He lost consciousness and became absorbed in the song..... At that movment he heard words.

"Raj, what is going on... the song is going on speaker, why are you singing so loudly... as if movie is going on... Where is your attention? "

While Raj was lost in the song, his mother came infront of him and said loudly...

By hearing his mother's voice Raj woke up as if waking up from the sleep, and become attentive... at that time song from "Sadma"... that song become reality song for his love story, stays with him continuously... same, " he Life ....meet me... he Life, meet me..."

As soon as the love story that started in Raj's mind came to an end, it was a coincidence with the music system in front of him ... so suddenly those memories came up and his eyes filled with tears...

Years have passed.... but even today, Raj goes to that Shiva temple and his eyes wander around looking for her ... and when he does not see her, he does not get sad as before.... As usual, he walks back to the temple of Lord Shiva, praying for his parents and her...

Raj has no choice but to accept the truth now ... because after so many years she must have married, she must be living a happy life in her new world ...So now there is no possibility to see her and even if she appears, time has gone ahead...

But maybe... Maybe she is still not married, then.... what to say.... maybe, it could be like that...?? Because, that divine miracle..... He still thinks that it has not been completed yet....So now,

Raj has not only hope but also firm faith, his Friday Valentine, that glorious love goddess... Once again with the same divine grace of Divine coincidence.... will return to Raj's life.... And his love saga will then be completed...

****

Credits

Thankfull to Blue Rose Team for published book on time & Special thanks to Dipank ji for Quick folows to complited all task before date. Always thankful to Author Vishal Ved Ji of FICTIO to guide every point of book publishing. Special Thanks to Abdul Razaq Ji of Minimalistmonk for making very atractive and meaningful book cover in a very short time.

Thanks to all.

Rajendra G

Introduction: Quality control in charge (SRK Consultant)

Laurels/Pride:

- In a personal letter from the Hon'ble President of India, Mr. Abdul Kalam addressed the issues of Sociology, Science, and Spirituality.
- Dainik Nawakal's public award for challenging writing from Honorable Journalist Editor Shri Neelkanth Khadilkar.
- A personal letter of congratulations and best wishes from the esteemed actor Mr. Amitabh Bachchan.
- Published notes on national interest and social reforms suggested from time to time from Dainik Loksatta, Maharashtra Times, Nawakal, Lokmat, etc.

9 789356 110380

Printed by Libri Plureos GmbH in Hamburg, Germany